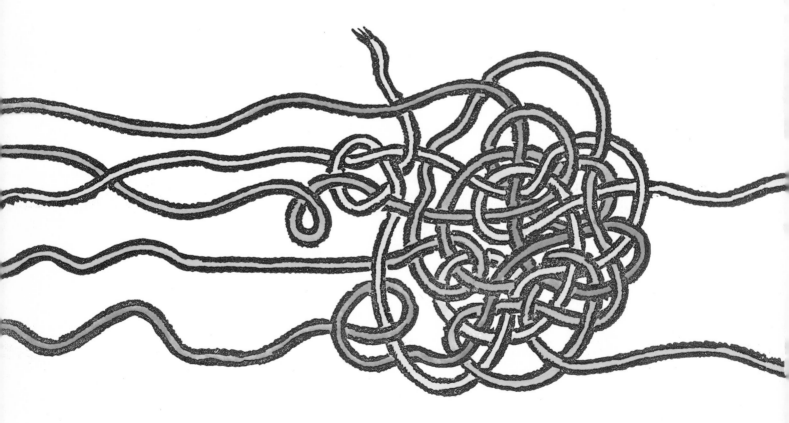

Tanglebird

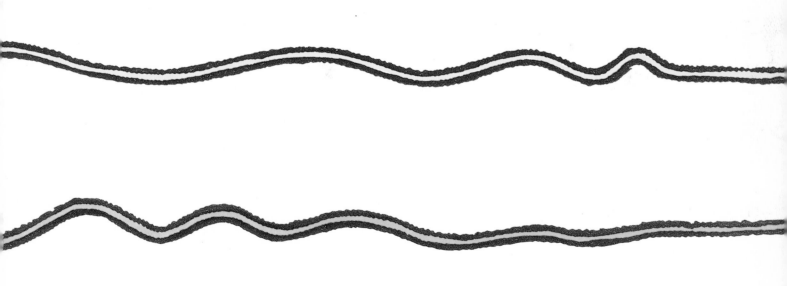

To Mum

Tanglebird

Bernard Lodge

Houghton Mifflin Company 1997

Deep in the woods the birds were busy
building nests. They used twigs and leaves and
they all made their homes as neat as baskets -
all except one.

This bird's nest was just a tangly mess.
The others called him Tanglebird.

The birds told Tanglebird to tidy up his nest.
But the louder they twittered and the faster
he worked, the more tangled his nest became.

The other birds screeched so much,
that they scared Tanglebird.
They scared him out of his tangled nest,
and right out of the tree.

Tanglebird flew out of the woods and
over the fields to the big city.

He looked for somewhere to build a nest.
But what could he build it with?
He had to find the right stuff.

He fluttered down to the city park
and perched on a bench.
Mrs Demarco sat there, happily knitting
a long, warm sweater.

"Wool!" thought Tanglebird.
"That will make a nice
warm woolly nest."

But Tanglebird didn't make a woolly nest.
He made a woolly tangle and tangled up
in the middle was Mrs Demarco.

"Wool is too soft," thought Tanglebird.
"I need something stronger."

He looked around and saw a long rubber hose.
"Great!" he said. "That will make a strong,
bouncy rubber nest."

But Tanglebird didn't make a bouncy rubber nest.
He made a terrible tangle of twisted rubber hose.
And tangled in the middle was the park keeper.

"Rubber is too bouncy," Tanglebird thought.
"I'll find something else."

Then he saw the kites!

"What a lot of ribbons!" thought Tanglebird.
"I can make a beautiful ribbony nest."
He flew up to the fluttering kites.

But he didn't make a beautiful
ribbony nest.

He made the worst tangle ever.
And who was tangled up in the middle?

Tanglebird himself!

The children were cross,
but one of them felt sorry
for Tanglebird.

Her name was Gina.

She worked at the tangle
of knots until Tanglebird
was free. He was too dazed
to fly away, so Gina took
him home with her.

"He can stay until he gets well," said Gina's father.
"Then he will want to fly home."

They fed Tanglebird on spaghetti. He loved it.
It was like a tangly nest of worms.

Tanglebird soon got better,
        but he didn't want to fly away.

Not yet.

Gina showed Tanglebird how to play
Cat's Cradle. He made a terrible tangle at first,
but soon he could do it well.

Then, Gina showed him how to tie knots and bows.
He became so good at it that whenever the
family needed a gift wrapped, they would
ask Tanglebird to tie the ribbons.

One day Gina's mother asked Tanglebird
to tie up a very special parcel.

It was Gina's birthday present –
a pair of bright green running shoes.
She tore off the paper straight away
and put them on.

Tanglebird threaded the shoelaces
and tied big double bows!

Next Gina showed him how to weave.
Weaving reminded Tanglebird of the tangly
nests he used to build and it made him sad.

He spent all his time looking out of the window,
because far away at the edge of the city,
he could see the woods.

Now Gina knew that Tanglebird was ready to fly home. She gave him a big bundle of coloured string and waved him goodbye.

Tanglebird flew out over the rooftops of the city towards the distant woods.

Deep in the woods, high up in the trees,
Tanglebird wove a nest of multicoloured string.

It was strong and warm and neat as a basket,
but much more beautiful!

Walter Lorraine *wx* Books

First American edition 1997
Originally published in Great Britain in 1997
by WH Books Ltd, an imprint of Reed Consumer Books Limited

Library of Congress Cataloging-in-Publication Data

Lodge, Bernard.
Tanglebird / Bernard Lodge.
p.   cm.
Summary: Unable to build a tidy nest without making a mess,
Tanglebird goes to the city and learns how to make wonderful
tangles and knots.
ISBN 0-395-84543-2
[1. Birds--Fiction. 2. Birds--Nests--Fiction.] I. Title.
PZ7.L8197Tan   1997
[E]--DC20   96-31030
                                                    CIP
                                                    AC

Printed in China
10 9 8 7 6 5 4 3 2 1